The Complete Adventures of

Big Dog and
Little Dog

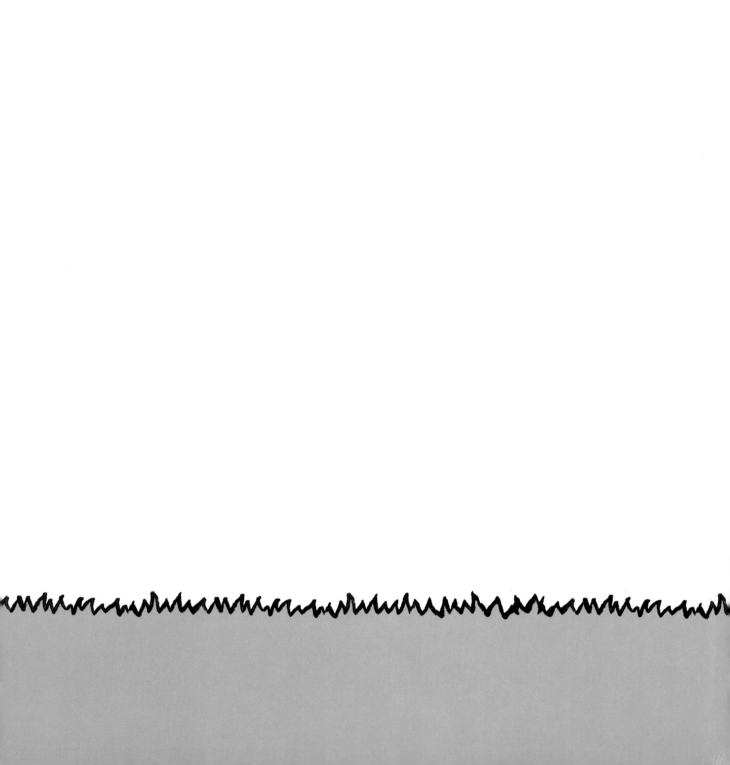

The Complete Adventures of
Big Dog and Little Dog

by Dav Pilkey

Harcourt, Inc.

San Diego   New York   London

Big Dog and Little Dog Making a Mistake copyright © 1999 by Dav Pilkey
Big Dog and Little Dog Wearing Sweaters copyright © 1998 by Dav Pilkey
Big Dog and Little Dog Getting in Trouble copyright © 1997 by Dav Pilkey
Big Dog and Little Dog Going for a Walk copyright © 1997 by Dav Pilkey
Big Dog and Little Dog copyright © 1997 by Dav Pilkey

www.HarcourtBooks.com

Library of Congress Cataloging-in-Publication Data
Pilkey, Dav, 1966–
The complete adventures of Big Dog and Little Dog/Dav Pilkey.
p. cm.
Summary: Big Dog and Little Dog eat, sleep, go for walks, and get into trouble.
[1. Dogs—Fiction.] I. Title.
PZ7.P63123Co   2003
[E]—dc21   2002007773
ISBN 0-15-204708-5

First edition

A C E G H F D B

Manufactured in China

To Nathan, Kevin, and Justin Libertowski;
Samantha and Bain Wills; Eamon Hoyt Johnston,
and Robert Martin Staenberg

Chapter 1

Big Dog and Little Dog

Big Dog and Little Dog are hungry.

Big Dog and Little Dog want food.

Here is some food for Big Dog.
Big Dog is happy.

Here is some food for Little Dog.
Little Dog is happy, too.

Big Dog and Little Dog are full.
Big Dog and Little Dog are sleepy.

Big Dog gets in the big bed.
Little Dog gets in the little bed.

Big Dog *is* lonely.

Little Dog is lonely, too.

Shhh.

Big Dog and Little Dog are sleeping.

Chapter 2
Making a Mistake

Big Dog is going for a walk.

Little Dog *is* going, too.

Big Dog and Little Dog see something.

What do they see?

Big Dog thinks it is a kitty.

Little Dog thinks so, too.

But it does not *smell* like a kitty.

Big Dog smells bad.

Little Dog smells bad, too.

Big Dog and Little Dog had a bad day.

They are going home now…

Chapter 3
Going for a Walk

Big Dog is going for a walk.
Little Dog is going, too.

Little Dog likes to play in the mud.
Big Dog likes to eat the mud.

Little Dog likes to splash in the puddles.
Big Dog likes to drink the puddles.

Big Dog and Little Dog had a fun walk.
They are very dirty.

It is time to take a bath.
Big Dog and Little Dog are in the tub.

Now it is time to dry off.

Big Dog and Little Dog shake and shake.

Big Dog and Little Dog are clean and dry.

Now they want to go for *another* walk.

Chapter 4
Getting in Trouble

Big Dog wants to play.

Little Dog wants to play, too.

But there *is* nothing to play with.

What will they play with?

Big Dog and Little Dog are playing.

They are playing with the couch.

Big Dog and Little Dog are having fun.

Big Dog and Little Dog are being bad.

Big Dog is making a big mess.

Little Dog is making a little mess.

Big Dog is in big trouble.
Little Dog is in big trouble, too.

Big Dog and Little Dog are sorry.
They will be good from now on.

Chapter 5

Wearing Sweaters

Little Dog has a sweater.

Big Dog does not have a sweater.

Big Dog is sad.
Big Dog wants a sweater, too.

Big Dog is looking for a sweater.
Little Dog is helping.

Big Dog has found a sweater.
Hooray for Big Dog!

Big Dog is putting the sweater on.

Little Dog is helping some more.

Now Little Dog has a sweater.

And Big Dog has a sweater.

Big Dog and Little Dog
are warm and happy.

Good night.

The illustrations in this book were done with acrylics and India ink.
The display and text type were set in Big Dog, created by Dav Pilkey.
Color separations by Bright Arts Ltd., Hong Kong
Manufactured by South China Printing Company, Ltd., China
This book was printed on totally chlorine-free Enso Stora Matte paper.
Production supervision by Sandra Grebenar and Pascha Gerlinger
Designed by Dav Pilkey and Barry Age